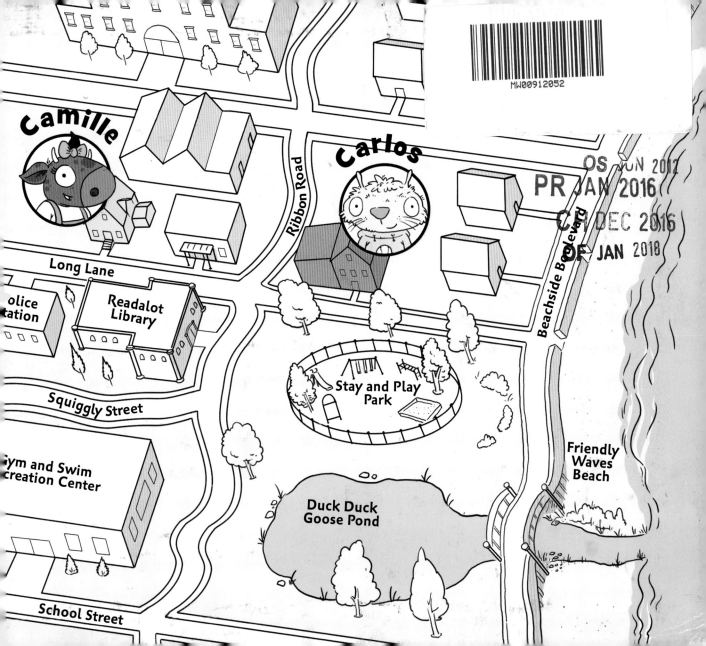

OUR CLASS

Stuart J. Murphy

Percy Listens Up

Social Skills: Listening

Stuart J. Murphy's
I See I Learn

ᴋᴀ Charlesbridge

Percy liked to talk.
He also liked to run and jump.

And he really liked to play.

Percy liked to play so much that sometimes he didn't listen.

One day Miss Cathy asked everyone to bring
a favorite toy to school.
But Percy was busy.
He didn't hear her.

The next day everyone had a toy.
Everyone except Percy.

"Nobody told me to bring a toy," said Percy.
"You weren't listening," said Miss Cathy.
"But don't worry. You can borrow one of our class toys."

listen to understand

At playtime Mr. D. taught everyone a new game.
Mr. D. explained the rules.
But Percy was busy.
He didn't listen.

The other children started to play.
Percy didn't know what to do.
"You're missing out, Percy!" yelled Freda.

"I'll teach you the rules so you can play, too, Percy," said Mr. D.

listen to learn

At the pool Percy's mommy said, "No running."
But Percy didn't listen.

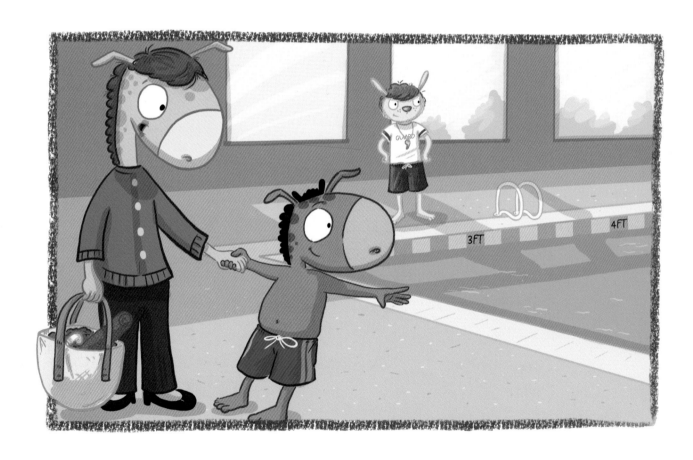

He started to run around the pool.
The lifeguard blew his whistle. "That's not safe," he said.
"Why?" asked Percy.

The lifeguard said, "You could slip and get hurt.
Or you might fall right in."
Percy listened to that!

listen to be safe

On Saturday Percy and his friends played at the park.
Camille's daddy said, "The ice cream truck is here.
Come on. I'll get you all a treat."

Freda heard him.
So did Ajay and Camille.
Percy was busy.

But Percy did hear the words "ice cream."
That got his attention.
Percy loved ice cream!

listen to join in

Percy's friends lined up to order their ice cream.
"I hope Percy heard Camille's daddy," said Ajay.
"He really likes ice cream."
"Here he comes now!" said Freda.

Just then Percy jumped in line.
"This time I listened!" he said. "Ice cream, here I come!"

listen to have more fun

Listen to:

learn

understand

be safe

A Closer Look

1. Are you a good listener?

2. Look at the pictures. What was Percy doing when he wasn't listening?

3. What happened when he did listen?

4. What are some things that can happen to you if you don't listen?

5. Ask two puppets to do something, such as put away their toys.
Show what happens when one puppet doesn't listen and the other one does.

A Note About Visual Learning and Young Children

Visual Learning describes how we gather and process information from illustrations, diagrams, graphs, symbols, photographs, icons, and other visual models. Long before children can read—or even speak many words—they are able to assimilate visual information with ease. By the time they reach pre-kindergarten age (3–5), they are accomplished visual learners.

I SEE I LEARN™ books build on this natural talent, using inset pictures, diagrams, and highlighted words to help reinforce lessons conveyed through simple stories. The series covers social, emotional, health and safety, and cognitive skills.

Percy Listens Up focuses on listening, a social skill. Listening shows respect for what other people have to say. Careful listening helps children understand directions, learn new things, be safe, and have more fun.

Listen up, everyone!

 Stuart